Text © 2018 Linda Ashman
Illustrations © 2018 Jamey Christoph

Published in 2018 by Eerdmans Books for Young Readers,
an imprint of Wm. B. Eerdmans Publishing Co.
2140 Oak Industrial Dr. NE, Grand Rapids, Michigan 49505

www.eerdmans.com/youngreaders

Manufactured in China

27 26 25 24 23 22 21 20 19 18   1 2 3 4 5 6 7 8 9 10

Library of Congress Cataloging-in-Publication Data

Names: Ashman, Linda, author. | Christoph, Jamey, 1980- illustrator.
Title: Outside my window / by Linda Ashman ; illustrated by Jamey Christoph.
Description: Grand Rapids, MI : Eerdmans Books for Young Readers, 2018. |
    Summary: "Children from all over the world describe what they see when
    they look outside their windows"— Provided by publisher.
Identifiers: LCCN 2017054360 | ISBN 9780802854650
Subjects: | CYAC: Stories in rhyme. | Neighborhood—Fiction. |
    Windows—Fiction.
Classification: LCC PZ8.3.A775 Out 2018 | DDC [E]—dc23
LC record available at https://lccn.loc.gov/2017054360

Illustrations created digitally.

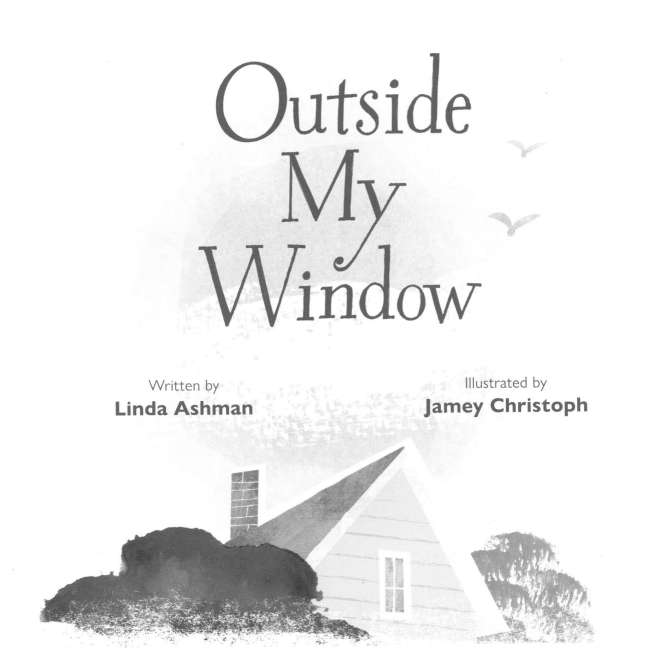

Outside My Window

Written by
Linda Ashman

Illustrated by
Jamey Christoph

Eerdmans Books for Young Readers

Grand Rapids, Michigan

Just outside my window
stands an old magnolia tree,
and hidden in its branches
is the tree house built for me.

What's outside *your* window?

Right outside my window
there are towers all around
and lots of tiny people
on the sidewalk way, way down.

I see a winding river
and mountains topped with snow.
I watch a freight train passing by
and hear its whistle blow.

Right outside my window
there are clouds above the plains.
I listen as the thunder booms
and wait for cooling rains.

I look out on the pastry shop,
its awnings white and red.
The people clutch their coffee cups
and wave batons of bread.

I see a busy boulevard,
where skinny palm trees sway.

An open gate, adobe walls,
the courtyard where we play.

Rows of houseboats just like mine,
tethered to the dock.

I see a narrow alleyway
and hear my neighbors talk.

I look out on a small canal,
pink with flowering trees.
I watch the ducklings paddle by
and feel the morning breeze.

A line of brownstone buildings,
grown-ups walking fast.
Strollers roll, pooches pull,
toddlers waddle past.

I see my father's garden,
his tidy rows of plants.
I hear the magpies chatter
and watch the poppies dance.

Just outside my window,
seabirds dive and soar.
Below them, foamy ocean waves
come tumbling toward the shore.

Looking out my window at this hour of the day,
the world outside your window seems so far away—
so far away and different from familiar things I see:
my neighbor's house, my little yard, the old magnolia tree.

But in the darkness of the night,
after I turn out the light,
I look up at the moon we share,
that shines in windows everywhere—

and then, somehow, the world feels small,
and you don't seem so far at all.

Author's note

I've always been fascinated by where people live—their homes, their neighborhoods, the climate and character of their town or city. We don't choose where we're born, and yet the sights, scents, and sounds outside our windows affect our lives in powerful ways.

Looking out someone's window—like "walking in someone's shoes"—helps us understand a person's life and circumstances. In writing this story, I hoped readers might imagine sitting at another child's window, viewing the world from his or her perspective. I also hoped the scenes of other people and places might pique their curiosity and give them a sense that there's a big world out there to discover.

Big . . . and yet not so big. Because regardless of where we live in the world, we all see the same phase of our one solitary moon each evening. Somehow, knowing that you and I can look out our windows at the same slim crescent or bright full moon tonight makes the world feel smaller—and our lives just a little bit closer.

— Linda Ashman

Illustrator's note

It was a thrill to create pictures for Linda Ashman's thoughtful words and help take young travelers on this world tour. As I sketched each scene, I wanted to make sure that children from every corner of the globe would be able to see themselves in the story.

It was also important that each place feel authentic. Gathering reference photos from books, postcards, and my own travels, I tried to capture those features, both iconic and less familiar, that make each location so special. I was inspired by some of my fondest memories—the New York City skyline, a cabin in the mountains, and the winding, narrow streets of Montmartre, Paris. I find it's the little details, unique to a place, that fascinate me most, like lampposts, trees, and patterns on fabric or a building.

Through social media, I have had the opportunity to share my illustrations from *Outside My Window* and make special connections with friends all around the world. I'm grateful for their feedback and our ongoing conversation. It's my hope that this book inspires you to make new friendships, near and far, and learn more about different places. Happy exploring!

— Jamey Christoph

Locations

Some of the homes in this story are located in particular cities; others can be found in specific countries or regions. Some may be near to you, while others may be very far away. There are children who live in almost every corner of the world—in more places than could ever be contained in one book.

New York, New York, USA

Rocky Mountains, Canada

Rural Ethiopia

Paris, France

Marrakesh, Morocco

Santa Fe, New Mexico, USA

Copenhagen, Denmark

Chichicastenango, Guatemala

Kyoto, Japan

Boston, Massachusetts, USA

Rural England

Nova Scotia, Canada